D0431832

DISCARD

E   C.1
Zolotow, C.
Peter and the pigeons.

DATE DUE	
MAR 0 1 2000	JUL 1 2 1997
MAY 0 9 2000	MAR 1 6 2005
AUG 0 9 2000	AUG 2 7 2005
NOV 0 4 2000	APR 0 8 2006
MAY 2 0 2001	
JUL 1 8 2001	
SEP 1 2 2001	
DEC 0 7 2001	
FEB 1 0 2002	
MAR 0 7 2002	
MAR 2 9 2002	
MAY 0 1 2002	
NOV 0 9 2004	
MAR - 8 2005	

GAYLORD   PRINTED IN U.S.A.

FEB 0 2 2006 GAYLORD

PETER AND THE PIGEONS

San Rafael Public Library
1100 E Street
San Rafael, CA 94901

by Charlotte Zolotow

pictures by
Martine Gourbault

Greenwillow Books, New York

Colored pencils were used for the full-color art.
The text type is Usherwood Medium.

Text copyright © 1993 by Charlotte Zolotow
Illustrations copyright © 1993 by Martine Gourbault
All rights reserved. No part of this book
may be reproduced or utilized in any form
or by any means, electronic or mechanical,
including photocopying, recording, or by
any information storage and retrieval
system, without permission in writing
from the Publisher, Greenwillow Books,
a division of William Morrow & Company, Inc.,
1350 Avenue of the Americas, New York, NY 10019.

Printed in Hong Kong by
South China Printing Company (1988) Ltd.
First Edition
10 9 8 7 6 5 4 3 2 1

Library of Congress Cataloging-in-Publication Date

Zolotow, Charlotte (date)
Peter and the pigeons / by Charlotte Zolotow ;
pictures by Martine Gourbault
        p.   cm.
Summary: After seeing all the animals in the zoo,
Peter still likes the pigeons he sees every day best.
ISBN 0-688-12185-3 (trade).
ISBN 0-688-12186-1 (lib. bdg.)
[1. Pigeons — Fiction. 2. Zoo animals — Fiction.]
I. Gourbault, Martine, ill. II. Title.
PZ7.Z77Pe   1993
[E] — dc20
92-29405   CIP   AC   C. 1

For Zee-Cat, Catullus, and Penelope
— C. Z.

For Charlotte and Christian
— M. G.

Peter loved pigeons.
He loved the soft, slow *cccooo-cooo*
sound they made and the
gray blue color of their feathers.

He loved the way they sat on statues and hid in the carved arches of church doors.

He loved to see them flying high and wild
in great sweeping circles in the sky,
and he loved to watch them
fluttering down again with a
flack-ack-ing wing sound.

He loved to feel the quick, sharp twitch
of their beaks as they took peanuts
from his hand.
They were his friends.

"If you love pigeons so much," his father said,
"we must go to the zoo. The zoo has strange
and unusual creatures. Tropical birds, and
wonderful, weird animals you don't see all the time."
Hand in hand Peter and his father went to the zoo
on a sunny Saturday morning. They walked
up the steps leading to the animals.

"Let's see which you like best,"
his father said.
The sun was warm on their heads as
they looked at the lion. He was huge
and golden against the green hill.
"He should be in a jungle," Peter said.

They saw a delicate, flowing-tailed red fox
with sharp, pointy ears and a quick, catlike
walk and fur that glinted in the sun.

"Him?" asked Peter's father.

"Not him," said Peter.

They watched the zebras a long time.
Like little striped ponies
they tripped back and forth,
stopping to nibble the
bright green grass.

Off in the corner was one baby zebra
who looked up straight into Peter's face.
"Him, I bet," said Peter's father.
"No," said Peter, though he smiled.
"Not him."

They watched the soft, lumbering,
white polar bears. One sprawled on a rock
by a waterfall and looked thoughtfully
at Peter and his father.

"Not you, either," Peter said kindly
to the bear.

They came to a pool where seals
with shiny black bodies and
small, whiskered, pointy faces
basked in the sunlight.
"These?" said Peter's father.
"No," Peter said. "Not these."

They saw a huge, wrinkled hippopotamus.

They saw a great gray elephant
with a long trunk and gentle eyes.
"Not these," Peter said.

When they had seen all the animals
in the zoo, Peter and his father
walked down the steps to go home.
On the last step a pigeon crossed in front of them,
puffing himself up like a feathery balloon.
He strutted over to a pool of pigeons
on the ground. They were fluttering
their wings and pecking at some crumbs.

A low, soft, cooing sound filled the air
as Peter and his father watched.
"I like pigeons best," Peter said.
"But you see them every day," said his father.

"That's why," Peter said. "I know their sounds
and even the feel of their feathers.
If I knew the others better,
maybe I'd choose them.
But right now, it's pigeons I like best!"